Snowflake Hollow - Part 1

12 Days of Christmas, Volume 1

Lexy Timms

Published by Dark Shadow Publishing, 2021.

This is a work of fiction. Similarities to real people, places, or events are entirely coincidental.

SNOWFLAKE HOLLOW - PART 1

First edition. December 1, 2021.

Copyright © 2021 Lexy Timms.

Written by Lexy Timms.

Copyright 2021 By LEXY TIMMS

ALL RIGHTS RESERVED. No part of this publication may be reproduced, stored in or introduced into a retrieval system, or transmitted, in any form, or by any means (electronic, mechanical, photocopying, recording, or otherwise) without the prior written permission of both the copyright owner and the above publisher of this book.

This is a work of fiction. Names, characters, places, brands, media, and incidents are either the product of the author's imagination or are used fictitiously. Any resemblance to an actual person, living or dead, events, or locales is entirely coincidental. The author acknowledges the trademarked status and trademark owners of various products referenced in this work of fiction, which have been used without permission. The publication/use of these trademarks is not authorized, associated with, or sponsored by the trademark owners.

All rights reserved.
Snow Flake Hollow
Part 1
12 Days of Christmas Series
Copyright 2021 by Lexy Timms
Cover by: **Book Cover by Design**[1]

---

1. http://bookcoverbydesign.co.uk/

12 Days of Christmas Series

Find Lexy Timms:

LEXY TIMMS NEWSLETTER:
https://www.lexytimms.com/newsletter
Lexy Timms Facebook Page:
https://www.facebook.com/SavingForever
Lexy Timms Website:
http://www.lexytimms.com

Want to read more...
For **FREE**?
Sign up for Lexy Timms' newsletter
And she'll send you updates on new releases, ARC copies of books and a whole lotta fun!
Sign up for news and updates!
https://www.lexytimms.com/newsletter

Snow Flake Hollow

THE BEAUTY OF CHRISTMAS lies not just in the date, but in the feeling it gives...

She's not the biggest fan of Christmas – which is akin to a major sin in the little town of Snowflake Hollow. And with a name like Holly White, it's fitting that she owns the only B&B in town. The whole season is a huge deal, and the people coming to stay at the B&B are paying a premium to get the ultimate festive experience. She's trying to keep the guests busy, but Hank the Handyman just broke his leg trying to hang the lights. Now she has to figure out how to make the holiday festivities happen all by herself.

Enter Lawson Lane.

Mister green eyes, tall, dark and handsome, has come home to see his mother over the holidays, and is surprised to see Holly as the owner of the B&B. When he notices her struggling to get things done, he offers a helping hand. Seeing Holly again and enjoying the holidays might take a

Christmas miracle—or he might end up with a lump of coal in his stocking.

It's 12 days of festive fun, what could possibly go wrong?

Lexy Timms brings you a Christmas holiday romance with 12 days of Christmas – each part of the story releasing like opening an advent calendar! Join in the holiday spirit with a festive read and some laughs to get you into the Christmas season.

Chapter One

Holly

CINNAMON ROLLS ARE supposed to make the house smell good. Everybody with even the slightest hint of holiday spirit has cinnamon rolls around Christmastime because they make the house smell all festive. Which was probably why my house currently smelled like a cross between potpourri and charcoal.

The biggest window above the kitchen sink was standing open, and I was using one of the kitschy towels I brought out for the season to desperately wave the smoke out into the fresh, sharply cold winter air outside. The towel was one of the things I found in the box my grandmother left behind in this sprawling place. I was sure the little white ruffle on the bottom of the red towel and the row of tiny black buttons along the front were supposed to be adorable.

I personally thought it looked like shrunken Mrs. Claus was decapitated, flattened, and dangled by a loop from the oven door. Somewhat different aesthetics happening there.

The smoke trickling out of the slightly open oven was fighting back, and I was waving with extra vigor to get it all out into the frosty morning rather than letting it get to the smoke alarm when I heard knocking on the front door.

From somewhere upstairs, a little boy's voice gave an excited yell.

"Santa!"

This was the third time the six-year-old had decided he was so important Santa Claus was going to set aside all his other holiday season obligations and visit him personally. His family had arrived two days before.

I heard Gregory's footsteps scurrying down the hallway and starting down the steps. Muttering a few choice phrases that were most definitely not the refrain of "Jingle Bells," I closed the oven door. I performed a few more frantic flaps of the kitchen towel toward the window, then tossed the towel aside and headed for the door.

Gregory was already there. His little hand reached for the handle on the door and pulled it open. His face immediately dropped when he saw Hank the Handyman standing there on the front porch with a bright grin on his face.

I probably would have thought his name was a joke if I hadn't grown up in Snowflake Hollow when his father Harry the Handyman was all the rage in the home improvement scene. Now, Hank was here to carry on the family legacy. Speaking mystically, of course. He was here—here being the massive gray Victorian-era house set on the small hill on a large plot of land—to help get me out of a festive season bind.

There was a stack of plastic totes behind him and a ladder leaned against the wraparound front porch that I was fairly certain weren't there when I got up that morning. So, I figured he was geared up for hanging my Christmas lights.

Well, not exactly my lights. Not technically, anyway. They were what was filling up all those totes behind him. They also weren't really mine because it wasn't like they were going on just my house. It was my house, technically, considering I lived there. But I didn't have the space to myself. That was because the big house I didn't even know my grandmother owned until she left it to me was actually a bed-and-breakfast.

That's right. I took my absolutely no knowledge of the hospitality industry, my questionable cooking skills, and a name I would always be just a little bitter toward my father for, and threw up a shingle as an innkeeper. Holly White, entrepreneur.

Right then, I was Holly White, frazzled, frustrated, and far from festive.

Fa-la-la-la-la-la-la-la-fuck all this nonsense.

The thing was, if I didn't own a bed-and-breakfast and was just hanging out in my own house, Hank the Handyman wouldn't be standing on my front porch waiting to deck the halls or anything else. There would be no lights. No wreath. No inflatables or bows or jingly anything. Nothing cheerful or seasonal. Nothing to remind me that Jack Frost was nipping at my nose and Christmas was nipping at my ass.

I was not a fan. There, I said it. The deep, dark secret that ranked right up there with murder in the town where I grew up. I just didn't like the holiday season as a whole. I'd much rather have my feet kicked up on a beach somewhere with the big green guy himself, drinking something fruity and tropical and eating nothing that involved cinnamon or peppermint.

Unfortunately for me and my sentiments, I was born and raised in the Christmassy-est place on Earth. And further unfortunately for me, I got swept up in my family loyalty after my grandmother's death and decided it would be a fantastic idea to open up a bed-and-breakfast just a few months before it was time to start welcoming guests for the holiday season.

It really did sound great at the time. Of course, "at the time" was in the summer when the snow was gone, there wasn't a twinkle light to be seen, and the closest thing to Santa I was dealing with was a caricature of him surfing across a window downtown for the Christmas in July sale. I was all sun-drunk and basking in the smell of hamburgers cooking on the grill and baseball playing on the TV. The idea of the holidays coming back and people actually coming to stay at the bed-and-breakfast seemed far in the distance.

And now here I was with less than a month to go, and none of the holiday season prep was done. Including decorating. Enter Hank the Handyman and his seasonal services.

"Thank you for coming," I said. "I know you're probably really busy this time of year."

The grin stayed firmly on his face as he shook his head. "Not really. Most everybody already has all their decorating done for the season. You're my first decorating job in two weeks."

"Of course I am."

"Besides, I'm excited to tackle this old place. I've been eyeing it since even before your gran bought it. There's so much potential. Do you have any particular vision for what you want it to look like? A theme or a style?"

"Christmas?" He laughed like he thought I was joking. Which was kind of adorable and sad at the same time. "Just go ahead and put the lights on however you think they're going to look best."

As I was saying this, the mail delivery truck showed up. I could already see a stack of packages on the seat and knew that meant there were even more tucked down beside her and possibly in the back as well.

"I'm going to get started," Hank said. "I'll let you know if I have any questions."

"Thank you," I said, starting down to help the mail carrier.

There was no need for her to try to juggle the entire assortment on her own. Especially considering how much lifting and delivering she was going to have to be doing over the next few weeks. I could only imagine how good of shape she was in by the time the holidays were over. If I was her, I'd probably admire it for a day or two, then blow it all on a couple of days locked in the house with milk and cookies.

That's one place Santa and I saw eye to eye.

They would definitely have to come from the bakery, though, because I wasn't the kind of woman whose kitchen transformed into a cookie factory as the clock struck midnight after Thanksgiving. Not in any kind of social commentary sort of way. Just in a lack of basic understanding of baking sort of way.

Which would be why as I climbed up the steps, unable to see over the stack of packages in my arms, I could hear the smoke alarm going off. Apparently, my smoke-waving efforts did not pay off fully.

I rushed into the foyer and resisted the urge to just drop the packages. There was no telling how many different ways these things could be breakable, so I lowered them carefully, then took off toward the kitchen. Bursting through the door, I found Mrs. Greene, a guest who had been with me for a few days by then, standing in the kitchen and staring at the oven door.

She was the age that made me absolutely positive she knew her way around one of these, and yet, she was staring at the glass front of the door like she thought it might take off like a spaceship at any moment. Which I could almost understand considering the glow of flame visible through the front.

Not only had she closed the door again, but she'd turned the heat back on, reigniting the already burned rolls.

"Thank you so much, Mrs. Greene," I said, trying my hardest to keep my voice calm and friendly. "I can take it from here. Why don't you go on out and keep working on those Christmas cards you've been signing the last couple of days? Yesterday you said you were just about done."

"Just twenty more," she said.

I nodded. "Go get 'em."

I kept grinning as she walked out of the kitchen. That woman's tongue was going to fall off when it came to stamp-licking time. Maybe I should cut up one of the extra kitchen sponges under the sink and soak it with water for her. On the other hand, she did have kind of a rhythm going. Stopping her from licking the stamps might ruin the whole Christmas card process. And she was responsible for further incinerating the rolls.

She smiled at me and gave a determined nod like I'd just given her the pep talk before the big game. Considering the massive stack of cards

I'd already seen her sign and address since arriving, the one activity she had actually done, I thought the comparison was apt.

As soon as the door closed behind her, I turned off the oven, opened the door, and jumped back to avoid getting taken out by the billow of smoke that poured out. The flames weren't nearly as big once I opened the door as I thought they were upon first glance. Which, granted, was still not a positive thing when talking about a kitchen appliance, but at least I wasn't in the middle of a recreation of *Backdraft*.

A few stiff smacks with the kitchen towel put out the small fire, and then it was all about handling the smoke.

The window was still mercifully open, so I was able to start wafting the smoke toward it the best I could. But this was going to call for more extreme measures. I rushed past the oven and through the door that led into the pantry. At the end was the back door, and I threw it open. Going back into the kitchen, I grabbed the headless Mrs. Claus towel and an oven mitt and started waving for all I was worth.

I had just found the groove in my smoke-removal flail when I heard a thud quickly followed by a shout. I paused. The smoke stung my eyes a little bit, but I was far more concerned about the second shout that followed quickly after the other, just after a decidedly metallic clang. That could not be a good thing.

I tossed the towel and oven mitt aside and ran through the back door, then around the side of the house to the front. The shouting was now groaning, and I followed it to Hank lying on the ground tangled in a strand of big multicolored light bulbs. His ladder was beside him. And his leg was at an angle no leg should ever be.

When the old poem talked about that clatter that arose out on the roof, this wasn't what they had in mind.

On the first day of Christmas, the Universe gave to me... a broken handyman and an insurance claim.

Chapter Two

Lawson

GROWING UP IN SNOWFLAKE Hollow was one of the greatest things to ever happen to me. Possibly the greatest thing. It sounds incredibly strange to say that, but it was true. My childhood in the tiny town was idyllic, and nearly all of my favorite memories still revolved around being there with my parents. I was an only child, but I never remembered being lonely or feeling like I was missing out on anything.

My mother and father were always doing something with me. I wasn't one of those children who came home from school to an empty house or spent breaks alone in my room or kicking cans down the alleys. Kids still did that, right? Maybe not, but the point remains the same. Snowflake Hollow was small and tight-knit, but that didn't mean it was boring. There was never a lack of things to do, and if my parents felt like we'd already done everything in the area enough or they just wanted to mix things up, they weren't afraid to jump in the car for an adventure.

I often wished I was as bold and outgoing as they were. These were the kind of people who would run outside in the middle of the night to catch the first snowflakes of winter on their tongues or slow dance in the middle of the grocery store aisle. I had the fantastic distinction of growing up kind of a nerd. I happily jumped into their adventures with them, but when I was in school, I didn't share their same zest. I was more likely to keep mostly to myself with a small group of friends and a lot of books.

That part might not have necessarily fit into that idyllic mold I was talking about. But it wasn't miserable. I would say my teenage angst quotient was kept to a minimum, and my college entrance essay didn't involve expounding on any trauma or massive hurdles I had to overcome.

Even after I left for college, I came back frequently to visit. I loved the feeling of Snowflake Hollow and the sense that no matter what I encountered or was dealing with in the outside world, I could come back here and feel like everything was alright. Sometimes I'd pack up friends from school and bring them back to have Thanksgiving dinner with us so they wouldn't spend the holiday alone.

And every one of them got to have the unique experience that was Snowflake Hollow at the holidays. Here, Halloween decorations didn't linger. Carved pumpkins, cobwebs, and ghosts were welcome, but come November first, they better be on their way back to storage to make room for the Christmas extravaganza that seemed to explode right after the last house with candy poured into a trick-or-treater's bag and turned off their porch light.

Harvest displays intermingled with early Christmas lights and garlands, and by the time Thanksgiving actually rolled around, there were more polar bears than Pilgrims making up the decorations around town. If there was one thing Snowflake Hollow always did right, it was Christmas. The whole season. I looked forward to it every year.

A lot of people think the whole magic of Christmas thing is only for children, but that wasn't how it worked in Snowflake Hollow. Everyone got wrapped up in the spirit and got that special twinkle in their eye. Groups of friends or families bundled up and drank cocoa while they caroled around the neighborhoods without a single shred of irony. People greeted them at the door with cookies. Children and adults alike made snow angels during the rare wintery storms. Whispers about Santa came from people of all ages, and while the parents would look at each other with those knowing winks, there were times when even they would have a flicker of belief. Here in Snowflake Hollow, magic was real, and it was for everyone.

It got harder after my father died. There was less sparkle in the air after that. But my mother and I tried hard to keep all the traditions alive. She kept decorating and doing everything she could, and I kept coming back to Snowflake Hollow. Through college and the first few years of my career, I came back a few times a year and always felt like I was coming home.

But after those few years without my father, when the loneliness really started to settle in, my mother decided she couldn't be in Snowflake Hollow without him anymore. She left and moved closer to her extended family, so that was where I started visiting.

It had been a few years since then, and I hadn't seen Snowflake Hollow since. My mother didn't want to worry me when her medical problems started getting serious, and she decided to move back to our town without telling me. I didn't know she was back until a few months back when she called to let me know that she was struggling on her own and had moved into an assisted living facility after selling the family home she'd kept for rental income over the years.

My mind spun when I heard that. I didn't get a chance to say goodbye to the house. I didn't get to help my mother move and settle in. It was like she'd made all these major decisions without me, and I felt left out of the entire process. But in a way, it didn't surprise me. That was Mom. She didn't like to cause trouble. She didn't like to feel like a burden to anyone. Especially me.

I'd been planning for my next trip to visit her to be at the holidays, so I just had to change where I was visiting. Now, I was back in Snowflake Hollow. It was a little bit surreal. After a lifetime of the town being like an anchor for me, I hadn't seen it for years, and now that I was back, it felt like I hadn't ever left. Everything was pretty much exactly the same as the last time I saw it.

There were a few little differences. A new business or two had cropped up. Some people had freshened up the color of their shutters or added a new lawn decoration. But it still gave me the same warm, nostalgic feelings. I could still name the families in most of the homes and had specific memories of the stores, restaurants, and other spots.

My car automatically went to the neighborhood where I grew up. I realized there was nowhere for me to go halfway down the street. The house was someone else's. I still slowed down in front of it, just to get another look. Whatever family bought it had already gone full-on with the decorations. It was missing something without the lights on since it wasn't quite afternoon yet, but I could see the potential. A flood of memories of my father washed over me. Decorating for Christmas was something he and I shared. My mother handled most of the inside of the house, but when it came to things like lights, signs, and inflatables, that was all Dad and me.

I could still see him planning out the lights starting in September, always wanting to try to improve on what he had done the year before. Then we'd get started in November. He made sure the lights were arranged in different sections that were individually operable so he could choose what to turn on each night. Throughout November, he would gradually turn on more and more every few nights. Then after Thanksgiving dinner, we'd have our grand illumination.

I smiled at that memory. It still stung a little bit, but that was alright. A little bit of ache and missing him in my heart was well worth all the joy and happiness it still brought me to think about him. It was a whirlwind finding out my mother was back in Snowflake Hollow and everything was so different, but now that I was here, it was all worth it.

I was home for the holidays. Even if it wasn't quite the same and felt a little strange, I was excited.

Giving one last look at the house, I drove out of the neighborhood and started across town. I'd made really good time with my trip into town, so I had arrived earlier than I expected. It gave me enough time to go by the bakery for some coffee and one of the incredible croissant sandwiches that showed up on the menu right around this time every year. Stuffed with turkey, gravy, and cranberry sauce, it was like filling an extra-buttery dinner roll with a holiday dinner and eating it straight from your hand. Essentially, nirvana.

When I finished my early lunch, I made my way toward where I was staying. The realization that without the family home, I didn't have anywhere to stay when I visited added to the overall shock of all the news from my mother. Especially considering Snowflake Hollow didn't even have a hotel. I didn't know quite what I was going to do. The thought of staying in a neighboring town went through my mind, but that wouldn't be the same.

That was when I heard there was a new bed-and-breakfast in town. As soon as I heard that, it made perfect sense. The town was adorable any time of year and a great place to visit, but at Christmas, it was a sight to behold. Tourists already came in from other towns just to take in the atmosphere and be a part of traditions like the annual outdoor market and fair. Having a bed-and-breakfast gave them a place to stay right in the midst of it all. And that was exactly what I was going to do.

I recognized where I was going as the GPS instructed me toward the far side of town. This was an older area of the Hollow, where big sprawling houses brought to mind generations before when wealthy people would come out of the cities to summer in the fresh, sweet air. Then they started coming for the holidays because it felt so much more personal and cozy. After a while, they just stayed, and Snowflake Hollow as a year-round town was born.

For the most part, these houses were still occupied by the same families who lived in them all those years ago. But there was one, the biggest and most impressive of the old-style mansions, that sat on a small hill looking out over a large plot of land, that had been empty for as long as I could remember. Turning it into a bed-and-breakfast was a perfect idea.

I pulled up in front of the White Christmas Inn and caught sight of something a little strange. A woman was up on a ladder leaned against the front of the house, struggling as she tried to hang an unruly strand of Christmas lights. I could already tell this was not going to go well for her, and I got out of the car as fast as I could. She was leaning precariously as I approached, and I could see she was definitely going to fall. I didn't want to startle her by calling out to her and possibly making the crash worse, so I just rushed toward her and opened my arms.

I managed to catch her right as she tumbled down.

"Hey," I said. "You're okay. I've got you."

The woman looked up at me and brushed a piece of hair away from her face. I couldn't believe it.

"Holly?"

Chapter Three

Holly

I'M DEAD. I'VE DIED and am lying on the ground, just like Hank the Handyman, only I hit my head on the way down and my brains are spilling out to join with the red lights I was hanging.

"Holly?"

And now I'm being celestially chastised for being too graphic near the holidays.

My eyes were squeezed shut as I braced for whatever came for people who accidentally smashed themselves preparing for Christmas and may or may not have uttered a lot of unflattering things on the way down. Then I realized I wasn't actually on the ground. I hadn't crashed down onto the grass but was being held in someone's arms.

Perhaps my guardian angel had been slacking just a bit but had gotten himself together fast enough to scoop me out of the sky before I turned into a really unfortunate Christmas-season newspaper headline.

I opened my eyes and looked up at the face looking down at me.

"Holly?"

This time I saw his lips moving at the same time I heard him say my name. Maybe I actually had hit my head on the way down. There was no way a gorgeous man with perfect facial hair and sparkling green eyes saw me about to fall, snagged me out of midair, and happened to already know my name. That was not my luck. My luck was my guardian angel was too busy spiking his eggnog to notice that I was tumbling off the roof like Thelma and Louise going over the canyon.

And yet, here he was, gazing at me like there should be music playing and maybe small children having a snowball fight behind us. In the no snow. At least I had that going for me this year. I wasn't having to deal with slush and cold and scraping windshields and shoveling and all the other things that came with wintery precipitation everyone else seemed to anticipate with such excitement.

The man slowly set me to my feet, and as I felt the cold ground under my boots, I realized that, in fact, I was not dead. I was very much alive. And very much embarrassed.

"Thank you," I muttered.

"No problem," he said. "Are you okay?"

I brushed myself off and nodded as I looked up at the man suspiciously. How did he know my name? Why was he impossibly handsome? How did he know I was going to fall? Why did he look like every guy in those terrible Christmas movies dominating just about every TV station right now, with his beanie and scarf and boots that didn't look like he'd picked them up on the clearance rack at the discount store.

(I did that. That was me. It occurred to me I was going to need them at some point and grabbed them on a whim. Add that to the list of bad decisions Holly made on a whim.)

The thing was, those men didn't really exist. They were actors, playing a part and otherwise living in Hollywood and probably sipping on fruity drinks in eighty-degree weather right now. They also didn't call me by name, ever. Maybe in my nightmares when I was questioning all my life choices, but not in real life. So unless this was a meta version of one of those movies during which I had gotten sucked into one and had to live it out, he couldn't be a seasonal hero.

Yet, here this man was, decidedly real and standing in front of me. It was the slightly expectant expression on his face that was getting to me a little. The beanie on his head was pushed forward a little bit, probably from catching me, but otherwise, he looked... perfect. Too perfect. Like the rest of the damn town the second November first showed up.

But that expression said he was waiting for something. It was the kind of expression people got when you ran into them and then realized you were supposed to be meeting them, or that you forgot a birthday or anniversary, or they thought you should know something and were waiting for you to say it, but you had no idea.

The more I stared at him, the more awkward the silence got, but at the same time the more familiar he looked. I was trying to figure out who he was, because if he knew me, I must have met him before. But I would certainly remember him checking in.

"It's Lawson," he finally said, pointing at his chest. Clearly this was the thing I'd forgotten, and he was waiting for me to remember. "Lawson Lane." Another pause. "From high school?"

At first, it didn't ring a bell. He might as well have said he was King Rudolph from Christmas-hell-dovia. But then it started to come to me. He was taller now and most certainly had filled out in ways I never would have expected for the artsy, quiet kid I remembered. He looked like he might have eaten the kid I remembered from high school as part of a protein shake that did really fantastic things for him.

"Lawson?" I asked. "What the hell are you doing here?"

Well, that wasn't very seasonally appropriate.

Or professional.

Or grateful.

I was really going for it.

He laughed, his wide grin stretching across his face in a way that somehow made him even more attractive.

"Catching you," he said.

I blinked at him a few times before I realized he was telling a joke.

"Oh. Ha," I said.

He laughed again. "I have a reservation at the bed-and-breakfast."

"You do?" I asked. "I thought you lived here. I mean not here, here. I know you don't live at the bed-and-breakfast. I thought you lived in Snowflake Hollow."

"I used to," I said. "But not anymore."

"Oh. Oh!" I said, slapping my forehead with my palm. "That's right, there was someone who hadn't checked in yet for today. Right. I'm sorry. That must be you."

"Yes," he said, looking a little confused himself now. "Are you working here?"

"Kind of. I own it," I said. "I apologize for not being ready for you. Hank the Handyman was over here doing all the lights and... he... fell. Broke his leg. Very terrible. Now I have to handle an insurance claim, which I guess makes me a real business owner now. Oh. And he's hurt, which, of course, is terrible. But... I'm babbling, so I'll just wrap this up."

"That's... a lot," Lawson said, grinning. "He broke his leg?"

"I think so. Unless he has some pretty exceptional flexibility that extends to his bones and joints going in the wrong direction," I said, trying desperately to stuff the words back in my mouth. Why couldn't I stop talking? "That's why I was up there. On the roof. With these."

I gestured vaguely at the lights now strewn over the ground nearby. They were tangled in tiny balls of hatred and electricity. One of them was responsible for wrapping around my foot and causing me to fall.

"That's awful," Lawson said.

"Yeah," I said. "I probably should have taken more warning from Hank. But I didn't. Thanks for catching me, by the way. That probably wasn't what you had in mind when you were thinking about checking in for your relaxing holiday getaway."

"Not exactly, but I was happy to do it," he said. "I'm just glad I got to you in time."

"How lucky," I said. "I mean, I'm lucky. I mean... let's get you checked in. Come on," I said. "These can wait."

For all eternity.

"Great," Lawson said.

"Do you need help with your luggage?" I asked.

He shook his head. "No, I can get it. Just give me a second. I left it in the car."

He headed for his car, and I took the time he was rummaging in his trunk to chastise myself. This was not the kind of first impression I should be making with guests. Owning a bed-and-breakfast might not be the most well-thought-out plan I'd ever come up with in my life, and it definitely wasn't going as smoothly as I would have hoped, but it was where I was in life.

This was what I was doing now. Forget all those things I used to say when teachers would ask what I wanted to be when I grew up. I was now the smiling face of hospitality. And I needed to make it work because I didn't have anything else going for me. It wasn't like this was some sort of passion project I was doing on the side while I kept up with a regular career like a sane person. I threw everything into getting this place off the ground, and now it was my only option.

Lawson got back to me, and we headed up the front steps onto the porch. I opened the door and stepped back to let him in first. He gestured for me to go ahead.

"After you," he said.

I didn't know why that gave me a little flutter in my chest, but it did. I went in and led him into the small alcove where I set up the desk. I went around behind it and got the computer system up and running so I could get him checked in. Scanning through the reservations, I found his.

"Yep, there it is. Lawson Lane. I don't know how that name didn't jump out at me when I was going over the reservations," I said.

"It's been a while," he said with a forgiving shrug. "And I'm probably not the only person in the world who has that name."

"I would venture to say you are the only person with that name who will ever stay in this bed-and-breakfast," I said, looking at the screen. "Alright, so it looks like you're going to be staying with us for a couple of weeks."

"Yep. Home for the holidays."

I looked up at him and gave a tight smile. "Very sweet." I took the guest book out from under the counter. This was one of the things I'd found with my grandmother's plans for the bed-and-breakfast. It was a large leather-bound logbook ready to be filled with the names and comments of guests. I opened it on the counter. "Would you mind signing this for me?"

"Sure. Do you have a pen?"

I opened the drawer beside me, and as I reached in, I heard some of the other guests who had come down and are gathered in the parlor off to the side of the foyer. I usually put out some snacks in the afternoons, but today things had gotten a bit out of hand, so I threw together a basket of packaged options and plopped it on the table before heading outside to tackle the lights.

"I was really hoping for more than this," one of them said. "The pictures made this place look like it was going to be the most amazing Christmas ever."

"I know," another responded. "I was expecting decorations and music and for the whole place to smell like cinnamon. And there's just... nothing."

"It doesn't feel like Christmas at all."

They were talking in hushed tones like they didn't actually intend on anyone hearing them, but one of the things about houses like this was they had great acoustics. Fantastic for the occasional thrown-together string quartet concert. Not so great for being subtle and keeping secrets.

I took the pen out of the drawer and held it out to Lawson with a sigh.

See? The house should smell like cinnamon.

Chapter Four

Lawson

HOLLY DIDN'T SEEM TO be having the best day. That was pretty obvious from the time I saw her toppling off the ladder with the Christmas lights wrapping themselves around her, but the sigh she just let out told me it wasn't that one isolated incident that had her frazzled and upset. I figured it very likely had something to do with the guests in the room behind me talking about how disappointed they were with the bed-and-breakfast. Or, more specifically, how disappointed they were with the lack of Christmas feeling there.

Not that I really blamed them. There was a distinct lack of seasonal spirit filling the home. There clearly weren't any lights on the outside, and I didn't see any decorations inside, either. There was no tree in the corner of the parlor that would be absolutely perfect for the purpose. There were no stockings hanging over the fireplace. Not even a garland or a piece of mistletoe to be seen.

Whether or not the house smelled like cinnamon was a bit up for debate. There was definitely a hint of something in the air that could possibly be associated with cinnamon, but it was acrid and bitter as well. Outside in Snowflake Hollow, it was like an enormous Christmas cracker had been torn apart right over the town. Inside here, it could have literally been any time of year. Well, any time of year other than Christmas.

But while I felt for the family who had likely thought this was going to be like walking into a postcard, it was the worn-down, discouraged look on Holly's face that was really getting to me. She was having a rough time, and I had a feeling it wasn't going to be getting better anytime soon. Every day, the holidays were getting closer, and that meant the expectations were just going to keep getting higher. These people were going to keep getting more eager, and she was going to be the one standing between them and the festive overload they thought they were signing up for.

I had the compulsion to try to make her feel better. She'd smiled at me outside, and while it was brief, I definitely wanted to earn another one. That smile was just as intoxicating to me as it was in high school. Probably more. Holly had grown up even better, which would have been almost impossible for my teenage self to imagine.

While she continued the process of checking me in, I glanced at the decorative plaque on the front of the counter that had the name of the bed-and-breakfast engraved into it.

"You did a really good job picking the name for the bed-and-breakfast," I said. I gave an exaggerated backward lean to demonstrate I was reading the plaque out to her. "White Christmas Inn, Holly White, proprietor. That's really cute."

I was hoping it was going to give her a bit of a boost to know someone thought she was doing something well. Instead, Holly gave a slight roll of her eyes and a nod.

"I didn't name it," she said. "It had that name even before I opened it. It's what my grandmother wanted to call it when she first got the idea. That wouldn't be what I would call it."

"Oh," I said, trying to rally. "What would you have called it?"

She ducked down behind the counter, and I heard a printer churning. "A big empty house with a lot of rooms." She came up with a printout in her hand and gave a discouraged sigh when she looked up from it and caught my eye. "I'm sorry. Again. As you might have just heard, this is the inn that stole Christmas."

"I guess you still aren't the biggest fan of Christmas?" I asked. She looked at me questioningly. "I remember your distaste for it when we were in high school. I seem to recall you lodging a protest against any decorations that referenced Christmas, refused to sing in the chorus purely because of the winter concert, and had the head cheerleader sent to the principal's office for bullying when she said 'ho, ho, ho' in your direction."

Holly let out a derisive snort and nodded. I chuckled, and she rebounded, stretching a massive put-on smile across her face and giving a big sweeping gesture with her hand.

"I mean, welcome to the White Christmas Inn. Where every day we're dreaming of a white Christmas."

She said it in her very best falsely cheerful advertising voice, and I playfully made a face.

"Meh," I said.

Her hand and expression dropped, and Holly shrugged. "I'll work on it." She grabbed a key off an old-fashioned pegboard behind her and came around the side of the desk again. "I'll show you to your room." We headed for the steps leading up onto the upper floors of the house. "All the guest rooms are on the upper floors. My wing is downstairs, and the room phones have a button that connects right to me, so if you need anything, you can get to me easily."

"Good to know," I say.

She glanced back over her shoulder at me, and I realized how that sounded. But she didn't say anything about it, so I didn't attempt to fix it. I likely would have just made it worse, anyway, so it was better to let it go.

"You booked one of the private bathroom suites. Good choice. But just in case there's someone else in your room and you need one, there are two shared bathrooms on each floor."

"Someone else in my room?" I asked, a little bit alarmed. I had not prepared myself for the possibility of making new friends quite that personally on this trip.

"I just meant if you had a visitor," she said.

There was a hint of suggestion in her voice that said she was trying very hard not to say she meant a woman I brought back to spend the night with me. I shook my head.

"There won't be any visitors," I said. "It's just me."

It seemed a little ridiculous that I was so eager to clear the air and make sure she understood my current relationship status, but somehow, her tiny nod gave me a sense of validation. High school me was apparently still alive and well deep in the back of my mind.

"Breakfast is served down in the dining room starting at eight every morning. It's served buffet style, so you're welcome to find a spot to eat it in one of the common rooms downstairs or bring it up to your room. I just ask if you do eat it up here you just bring the dishes down to the kitchen when you come back down for the day." We got to my room, and she used the key to open it up. She stepped inside and opened her arm to welcome me in. "Here you go."

I look around, taking in the room. It might not have been bursting with Christmas spirit, but it certainly had the quaint, cozy feeling a bed-and-breakfast was supposed to have. There was even a fireplace to one side and a rocker with what looked like a handmade blanket draped over the back nestled into the picture window overlooking the backyard.

"This is great," I said.

She nodded, glancing around. For the first time, there was something that looked like happiness and even pride on her face.

"It's probably my favorite of the guest rooms. It's not as big as the rooms I use for families, but it has the best window and the fireplace. That desk over there is also original to the house. It was here when my grandmother bought it."

"Wow. That's awesome," I said.

She nodded again, then seemed to go back into her professional innkeeper mode. "Towels and washcloths are in the closet in the bathroom. Just leave the used ones outside your door, and I'll get them. There's an extra set of bedding in the closet and a couple of extra blankets in case it gets really cold. Do you think you'll need another pillow?"

I looked at the bed and counted four. "No, I think I'll be okay."

"Okay. Well, I like to think of this as a home rather than something like a hotel, so I avoid coming into the rooms. Housekeeping is offered once per week, but you're welcome to fresh towels or linens whenever you need them. Just call and I'll get them to you. There are some books on the shelves if you feel like reading. Downstairs, there's a library with a lot more books. The living room has a fireplace and TV. There's a sitting room with puzzles and games. The sunporch on the back of the house is a really nice place to sit. I serve snacks in the parlor each afternoon.

"Other than that, there aren't a lot of activities or anything here. I figured most people are visiting here so they can spend time in Snowflake Hollow, which has so much going on all the time, especially at Christmas. You shouldn't miss the lights tours or the decorations down Main Street. The Christmas Faire is coming up. That is a favorite activity around here. There are games and food, an artisan market…"

"Holly?" I said, stopping her spiel. "I know. Remember? I grew up here. My parents used to have a booth at the market each year."

"Right," she said with a single nod. Her lips rolled in on each other, and she seemed to bite down on them as she looked around the room for something else to talk about.

I realized then that this woman had no real memories of me from high school. Some might exist somewhere on the very edges of her mind, but I doubted they had a lot of impact on her. I couldn't really blame her. She was in a whole different realm than I was when we were in school. She was one of the popular girls, all of her attention getting poured onto the quarterback she was dating. She didn't really fit in with most of the people of that crowd, but she was smart, beautiful, and seemed good at everything, so she was naturally at the top of the hierarchy.

I was not.

"Is there a time when the front door is locked so we can't get back in?" I asked.

I didn't really need to know, and I felt like I'd chosen probably the most ridiculous question I could have, but something needed to fill up the silence and stop her from how awkward she obviously felt.

"No," she said, shaking her head. "There's an electronic lock on the front door. The keypad has a code that will unlock the door anytime. 1225." I did my best not to laugh at her, but she saw me biting my lips to stop it and nodded. "I know. But it's easy to remember. It's also Snowflake Hollow, so I could just prop the door open and leave it that way all the time and nothing would happen."

"That's probably true," I said.

"Do you need anything? Anything else that could make your stay comfortable?" she asked.

I knew it was probably something she asked everyone who checked in, but I liked it anyway. I shook my head.

"No. I think I've got everything," I said.

"Good. Well, then I'll leave you to settle in. If you think of anything, let me know."

She stepped out of the room and closed the door behind her. I hesitated for a second, then set my luggage down and started unpacking. It didn't feel great knowing Holly didn't really remember me, but at the same time, I was fully aware how silly it was for me to feel that way. We weren't friends, I never did anything impressive enough to really stand out, and it wasn't like I ever told her about my crush on her.

I'd thought about it so many times. I fell head over heels for her the second I saw her, and it never faded. There were plenty of times when I thought it was just going to drive me crazy if I kept holding it in and not doing anything about it. Even though I knew she was going to reject me off hand and it would probably be the most embarrassing moment of my life, I would have at least gotten it off my chest and wouldn't have to carry it around with me anymore. That rejection might have been just what I needed to get over the crush and think about something else.

But telling myself all those things was a whole lot easier than actually gathering up the courage to do them. And that part never came about. I couldn't bring myself to walk up to the quarterback's girlfriend and tell her I had feelings for her. This was the girl who sat beside the most popular, powerful, and influential guy at school in the convertible during the Homecoming parade. The one who got dressed up and went to every Friday night football game so when the team won, he could bring her down onto the field and make a big show out of kissing her in front of everyone.

They were the golden couple. Everyone saw them going far in life. Everyone but those of us who could see right through the guy and knew he was trouble. Good-looking and wealthy, sure. But also arrogant, indulged, and tainted by the kind of parenting that told him he was the very best at everything he ever tried, was always right, and could have and do anything and everything he ever wanted.

I didn't see expressing feelings toward his girlfriend would go over particularly well. Instead, I just relied on the possibility of her figuring it out for herself. I figured it was obvious since I was so incredibly into her, and being smooth was never really my strong suit. But she was so wrapped up in her quarterback it was like she didn't know anything else even existed in the world.

That was part of the reason I was so surprised she was there. The last thing I knew about Holly, she'd never come back to Snowflake Hollow after leaving for college. I told myself it didn't really matter. I was just here for a visit, and I hadn't even known she owned the place when I made the reservation. It wasn't like I was here specifically to be near her again.

I finished unpacking and called my mother to let her know I'd made it. She told me she couldn't wait to see me, and right as I was telling her I would come see her soon, I heard a loud crashing sound coming from outside.

"I've got to go, Mom. See you soon. Love you," I said.

I got off the phone before she even responded and rushed to the window. I couldn't see anything, but when I opened a segment of the picture window and leaned out, I could most certainly hear Holly. Rushing out of my room, I rushed downstairs and looked out through the long glass panels positioned on either side of the door. I could see Holly flailing around, kicking lights tangled around her again and the ladder on the ground.

Chapter Five

Holly

I WAS GOING TO NEED to invest in some soundproofing for one of the easily accessible downstairs rooms at the bed-and-breakfast. When I was having a day like the one I was having, shouting out "sugar plum fairies!" didn't have quite the zip I was looking for. I needed an escape room where I could lock myself for brief periods of time to flail around and say all the things I really didn't want my guests to hear me spouting off.

After hearing the scathing review of the inn from those guests, I decided I really did need to get a move on with the whole preparing for the holidays thing. I couldn't let my first season also be my last. This might not have been the very best idea I'd ever come up with in regards to my future, but it definitely wasn't the worst, either. At least this had some chance of viability if I could get myself together enough to make it work.

That was the thought that made me head back outside after leaving Lawson in his room. These lights weren't going to win. A strand of multicolored light bulbs wasn't the boss of me. I was the boss of them. They were going to get in place on the house, light up like a magical freaking wonderland, and give these people the holiday of their dreams.

As determined as I was when I marched back out there, all the mantras in the world weren't going to save me from the lights. I was back to fighting with them as if they somehow knew I was a traitor who couldn't wait for this whole thing to be over when Lawson came out onto the porch. None of my other guests seemed to notice I was in a battle for my soul against some twinkle lights. Or they just didn't care. Which wasn't very Christmassy of them. But Lawson looked concerned.

"I thought you'd given up on the lights," he said.

"I didn't give up on them," I said. "I fell away from them. But I still need to get them up."

Glaring at the ladder, I decided getting that standing properly could be the first step in an effective light-hanging strategy. I dropped the lights and went over to the ladder to get it back in place.

"Would you like some help?" Lawson offered.

"Nope," I said. It came out as somewhat of a grunt as I wrestled the ladder into place. "You aren't here to work. You're here to relax and enjoy your holidays."

I got the ladder into place and let out a breath, brushing my hair back over my forehead.

"No," he said, coming down the steps toward me. "Actually, I'm here to visit my mother. Besides, you look like you're having a rough time, and I'm taller. I have more of a reach without having to lean. And I even have some experience hanging lights. Just let me help you."

He reached down for the lights, and I watched as he started untangling them and wrapping them into a large loop around his hand and elbow. Maybe my mantra had drifted into the house and gotten to him, because he was certainly determined not to let me be the only one messing with the lights that day.

"You know, not for nothing, but the last two people who tried to wrangle those lights ended up falling off the ladder," I said.

He grinned at me. "Clark Griswold did, too."

I shook my head. "That is not really an argument in favor of your side. He isn't really the ultimate in Christmas success icons."

"But his house ended up being the best one on the block, right?" Lawson said. "And by the end, he had everyone in the front yard, singing and celebrating, and they thought it was the best old-fashioned family Christmas they ever had."

"It was the only old-fashioned family they ever had," I said. "That was kind of the entire purpose behind the movie."

"And the point of the Grinch isn't that he stole Christmas, is it?" he asked.

Damn. That was a good one.

"Alright," I said. "Go ahead."

He grinned and headed up the ladder with the lights slung over his shoulder. I braced myself, not sure if he fell I would be able to return the favor of rescuing him. But he didn't seem to need my help. He got right to the top step of the ladder, obediently respecting the note on the very top that said it wasn't a step, and started stringing up the lights. I'd managed to spend enough time on the ladder that I'd gotten the staple gun up on the roof, so he snagged it, and within what seemed like a few seconds, he already had the whole distance he could reach to either side securely strung.

"Tell me you have more lights than this," he called down to me.

"Oh," I said, nodding. "Yeah. I have plenty."

I gestured over to the stacks of plastic totes Hank brought but that had never gotten as far as to be unloaded.

"Perfect. Bring me some," he said. "Not going up and down dramatically reduces the risk of falling off the ladder."

He chuckled, and I flashed him a thumbs-up.

"Good tip." I went to the stack of totes and disassembled it so it was just a row across the grass. I popped the tops off all of them so I could look inside and see what I was working with. "What kind do you want?"

"What do you mean?"

"It looks like I have white ones and colored ones and little ones and big ones."

"Well, options are always useful. But I think we should probably go with the same kind that I've already strung if you want to go for a traditional look. If you want to get avant-garde with it..."

"No," I said, shaking my head as I pulled out several more coils of lights and handed them up to him. He looped a couple over his shoulder and set the rest on the roof. "No, I do not. I am going for real Christmas. You are familiar." I made a swirling gesture with one hand to encompass the entire building. "Just do... that." I started inside, then scurried back down the steps. "Are you okay out here by yourself for a minute? You don't need me to hold on to the ladder or hand you more lights or anything?"

"No, I'm good. It's a good, stable ladder. I should be able to handle it," he said. I was at too far of a distance to be positive, but I was pretty sure I saw a twinkle in his eye when he said it.

"Okay, because I was just going to go inside and set out some apple cider and snack mix in the parlor. But if you need me to be here to... assist in any way, I'll stay," I said.

Lawson shook his head. "You go ahead. I have enough lights here to handle the rest of the porch and probably at least one side of the house. Then I'll move over to the other and the back."

"That sounds like a lot of work. You really don't have to do it," I said. "I could probably find another handyman somewhere. There has to be a Harold or a Henrich or something around here or maybe in the next town."

He laughed, continuing to put up the lights with no sign of instability or potential falling. "Don't worry about it. I'm having fun."

I hesitated, waiting for him to change his mind. When he didn't, I went in and headed for the kitchen to get out the snack for the afternoon. I hauled a slow cooker into the parlor and set it up on a card table rather than putting it on one of the pieces of antique furniture. Plugging it in, I filled it with apple cider and spices, then went back for the snack mix. I put it in a large ceramic bowl decorated with snowflakes and set it out on another table with napkins, ramekins, and cups.

When I was finished, I filled a cup with the cider and a ramekin with the mix. The cider hadn't had a chance to warm up yet, so I brought it back into the kitchen for a zap in the microwave before carrying it outside to Lawson. He was coming down the ladder as I walked out, and I held the snack out to him.

"Here you go," I said.

He smiled as he accepted it. "Thank you. Is this my version of room service?"

"You're taking all this time to string my lights for me. I figured the least I can do is bring you a snack."

He took off his gloves and filled his palm with the snack mix. Tossing it back into his mouth, he chewed for a second, then gave a nod of approval.

"This is delicious," he said.

I shrugged. "It's just various cereals mixed with copious amounts of butter and packets of seasoning I get at the grocery store. But just the smell of it reminds me of Christmas. It's one of the few things that does that to me that I actually don't mind so much. My grandmother used to make it every season. Technically, the recipe includes pretzels and peanuts, but she always used to say she didn't have time for all that mess. She was straight-up cereal, and that was just the way it was."

Lawson chuckled and ate another handful before sipping his cider. He finished his snack, then headed back up the ladder to finish up. He made quick work of the rest of the lights, and soon we were standing back to admire the lights. Albeit unlit lights, but lights nonetheless.

"They'll look better in the dark," he said.

"I'm just glad they're there now," I said. "Thank you. Really. I appreciate it a lot."

"It wasn't a problem. I was glad to be able to do it for you."

We started inside, and just as I was closing the door, the big grandfather clock in the foyer chimed. Lawson's eyes snapped to it.

"Everything okay?" I asked.

"Yeah," he said, digging his phone out of his pocket to compare the time on the clock and the one on the screen. "I just didn't realize what time it was. I need to get over and see my mom before it's too late in the day."

"Okay. I'll see you later," I said.

He smiled. "See you later.

I watched him leave. Why was I just now noticing this man? Why couldn't I have just noticed him while we were in high school rather than wasting all my time on the jerk quarterback who monopolized me all four years and then dropped me as fast as he could when something he thought was better came along.

The sound of the smoke alarm blaring inside again broke my musings. My head fell back, and I closed my eyes, hoping for a moment of serenity. It didn't come, so I settled for a few more creative Christmas-themed curses as I rushed inside. I found Mrs. Greene standing in front of the oven again. This time, the smoke was spiced cereal-scented.

"Hi, Mrs. Greene," I said. "Is there something I can help you with?"

"I thought it would be nice for the snack mix to be warm," she said. "Do you think I put it up high enough?"

She had it on the high broil setting.

I shooed her out of the kitchen as diplomatically as I could and worked on getting the smoke out as I contemplated the merit of a padlock on the kitchen door. I was sure I could come up with a creative way to make it look less foreboding.

Chapter Six

Lawson

I DIDN'T KNOW EXACTLY what to expect when I went to the assisted living facility to visit my mother. She'd told me about it and always seemed happy when she described the amenities or the friends she made. But there was the worry in the back of my mind that she was just saying that to make me feel better because she knew how upset I was that she'd done all this by herself. I worried I was going to show up and it would be run-down and miserable, that she would not be getting the treatment she deserved or that she would be spending all her time alone.

I also worried her health was far worse off than she'd told me. I didn't want to think she was suffering or that her condition was deteriorating, and she was waiting for my Christmas visit to tell me, but I didn't know. I never would have thought she would have sprung something like selling the house and heading into a facility on me, either.

As much as it upset me, it wasn't like I was mad at her for the decision she'd made. It was hers to make, and I didn't have any say in it. My mother deserved to do what was right for her regardless of what anyone thought. I couldn't even imagine what she had gone through already with losing my father and then facing the series of medical issues that brought her back to Snowflake Hollow and eventually into the facility. There was no way it was an easy decision for her. It would be beyond selfish of me to think I should be allowed any emotion surrounding it or how she made it.

I just wanted to know she really was safe and happy. And that I didn't need to be so worried about her all the time. My mother was what I had left in this world. She had always encouraged me and made sure I had every opportunity possible. She made sure I knew I had the ability to pursue my dreams and make them happen. Wanting to be able to take care of her and give her a good life was one of the reasons I worked so hard to get where I was.

It was a pleasant surprise when I went into the facility with her. It was beautiful and welcoming, very different from what I had in my mind. I found her in a common room with several other women, laughing and talking as they played cards. She looked as happy as she told me she was. Maybe a little more tired than I would like, but happy.

Her face lit up when she saw me, and I met her with a hug. She felt a little more frail and a little weaker than the last time I saw her, but she was smiling and seemed like she felt good. She immediately brought me over to her friends to meet them, then led me to her little independent apartment. We spent the next few hours sharing memories and visiting. It felt at once like it had been years since we'd seen each other and like we had just been together a couple of weeks before.

I stayed until late in the evening. Mom didn't want me to leave, but it was obvious she was exhausted and just needed her rest. As she turned on her favorite evening TV show and sipped at her favorite cup of tea, I kissed her head and promised I would be back to see her soon.

It was dark by the time I pulled up to the bed-and-breakfast. The lights were glowing, and it looked much more welcoming than it had. There was still room for improvement, but I wasn't worried. That could be taken care of easily.

Walking up to the house, I noticed Holly sitting in one of the white gliders on the front porch, wrapped up in a blanket. She lifted a mason jar to her lips as I climbed the steps and let out a little sigh, nuzzling deeper into the blanket as she swallowed.

"Hey," she said. "How's your mom?"

"She's good," I said. "I really like the place where she's living. She seems happy."

"That's good to hear." She took another sip.

"What are you drinking?" I asked.

Holly lifted the glass and looked through the side into it as if she had forgotten what she'd put in there.

"Hot spiced alcohol," she said.

I laughed. "You probably deserve it after the day you had." She lifted the glass toward me like she was making a toast to the fact that the day was almost over. "Mind if I join you?"

"Go ahead," she said, gesturing to the other pieces of furniture on the porch.

I chose a chair to the side of the glider and sat down. It was a cold night, but I was still bundled up in my coat, gloves, hat, and scarf, so it didn't bother me much as I sat there with her. It was nice to just enjoy the glow of the lights and the fresh air. We sat there in silence for several seconds, and Holly was the one to finally break it.

"How did you know I don't like Christmas?" she asked.

"I told you, I remembered those things you did in high school," I said.

"I know," she said. "I just mean, how do you remember that?"

I shrugged, looking out over the yard again for a moment before meeting her eyes again.

"It just stood out to me. Everyone would always get so excited when Christmas was coming up. They wanted to participate in the festival or the market, or they were just planning on going and talked about what they were going to wear and who they were going to go with for weeks leading up to it. But you never did. You never wanted anything to do with it, and I remember you actually refusing to participate in things even when the clubs you were a part of had something to do there," I said.

Holly sighed, looking down in her cup for a second. "That makes me sound really terrible."

"No, it doesn't. You don't have to be a rabid fan of Christmas in order to be a good person. And it doesn't make you a terrible one to not want to participate in the same things as everyone else." She still looked sad, so I gave a shrug and leaned back in my chair. "I mean, I did hear from a couple of people that you were known for snapping candy canes in half and kicking plastic Santas on people's lawns. That's kind of mean."

"Candy canes are offensive to shepherds, and those Santas had it coming," Holly said with a straight face. We looked at each other and chuckled. She shook her head and let out a breath. "I don't know. I just never liked it. Even as a kid. It's not like something super traumatic happened that tainted Christmas for me or anything. I do have some really happy Christmas memories from when I was little. When I got older, it just wasn't as much fun, and it started to feel so forced and artificial. It was like everybody went off into this weird fantasy world and forgot about reality for a while."

"And that's a bad thing?" I asked.

She looked at me strangely. "Forgetting about reality? Yes. I would say that's a bad thing."

"I don't think so. I think it would be awful to not have the chance to escape reality, at least for a little while every now and then. That would mean no movies. No TV. No theme parks."

"Those are different than being obsessed with an entire season. Acting like everything is so magical and special and heartwarming when it's the same stuff that happens every single year," Holly said.

"It's not acting if they really feel it. And just because something happens every year doesn't mean it's not magical. In fact, I think that having a chance to look forward to things and enjoy them every year is magical on its own," I said. She nodded but didn't say anything. "How did you get wrapped in a bed-and-breakfast, anyway? It doesn't seem like something you'd be into."

"That would be accurate," she said. "And I didn't choose it. Not exactly, anyway. Well, I guess I did, but not because I wanted to. I don't know if you know that my grandmother raised me."

"I think I remember that," I said.

"Alright, well, she did. And she was amazing. She even understood when I told her I didn't want to come back to Snowflake Hollow after college. She wanted me to go out into the world and find my own way. Find what was going to make me happy. So, I did. When she died earlier this year, I came back to settle everything. I found out she bought this place. I had no idea. She never talked to me about it. Probably because I would have told her I thought opening a bed-and-breakfast was a crazy idea for someone without any experience doing something like that.

"I found all these plans that she'd made and her journals with notes in them talking about everything she dreamed about for it. It really was a huge dream for her. It was something she wanted so much but wasn't ever able to achieve. So, I decided to do it for her. I was going through kind of a transitionary period in my life anyway and thought this would be a great way to get a fresh start. I wanted to make sure my grandmother's dream comes true so people can come enjoy the wonderland of Snowflake Hollow if that kind of thing is their jam."

I laughed, but there was also a little lump of emotion in the middle of my chest hearing her talk about her grandmother and what she was willing to do for her. I was impressed by Holly and even more glad I was staying at the White Christmas Inn. I already had the inkling I wanted to make this season easier for her, but right then, I decided I was going to do everything I could to show her that Christmas didn't have to be something she dreaded. I was going to help her make and keep her guests happy.

We stayed out on the porch a little longer before Holly announced she needed to get to bed. I walked inside with her and said good night, then headed up to my room. After a shower, I slipped into bed and fell asleep, feeling optimistic about the next day.

THE END
OF

PART 1

Snowflake
HOLLOW
12 DAYS OF CHRISTMAS
ADVENT CALENDARS
3
12
7
5
10
9
2
4
6
1
8
11
NEW CHAPTER EVERY DAY

Find Lexy Timms:

LEXY TIMMS NEWSLETTER:
http://www.lexytimms/newsletter
Lexy Timms Facebook Page:
https://www.facebook.com/SavingForever
Lexy Timms Website:
http://www.lexytimms.com

Want

FREE READS?

Sign up for Lexy Timms' newsletter
And she'll send you updates on new releases, ARC copies of books and a whole lotta fun!

Sign up for news and updates!
http://www.lexytimms/newsletter

Holiday Romance by Lexy Timms

LOVERS IN LONDON SERIES #6
Sparkling
CHRISTMAS
USA TODAY BESTSELLING AUTHOR
LEXY TIMMS

DRIVING HOME FOR
Christmas
LEXY TIMMS
LIMITED
TIME
Lexy
Timms
FREE
DOWNLOAD

Fake
BILLIONAIRE
SERIES
Fake
CHRISTMAS
USA TODAY BESTSELLING AUTHOR
LEXY TIMMS

BUTLER &
HEIRESS
SERIES
All
Wrapped
Up
USA TODAY BESTSELLING AUTHOR
LEXY TIMMS

Don't miss out!

Visit the website below and you can sign up to receive emails whenever Lexy Timms publishes a new book. There's no charge and no obligation.

https://books2read.com/r/B-A-NNL-GLLTB

BOOKS 2 READ

Connecting independent readers to independent writers.

Did you love *Snowflake Hollow - Part 1*? Then you should read *Driving Home for Christmas*[1] by Lexy Timms!

USA Today Bestselling Author, Lexy Timms, shares a holiday romance that'll warm the heart and having you wishing on love—or beating it with a stick!

Colin Murphy Is the CEO of Murphy Inc and is a workaholic. Christmas, or any holiday in face, doesn't mean much to him. When his business trip travel plans get interrupted by a freak snowstorm, he's forced to find a way home by other means.

Abigail Thompson can't wait for this year to be over. After losing her job, her boyfriend and apartment, she's ready to go home for a much-needed break and to regroup. But when her plane is grounded because of a snow storm, she has to find another way. She makes her way to the car

---

1. https://books2read.com/u/bOaWRA

2. https://books2read.com/u/bOaWRA

rentals only to find the last car has just been given to a tall dark sexy man. Definitely not Santa, his name is Colin Murphy. When Colin finds out they're head in the same direction, he offers her a lift. It's nearly Christmas afterall.

What should be an easy 8-hour drive turns into 2 days of mishaps and mayhem.

She knows every Christmas song off by heart, even though she can't carry a turn. She's happy, he's a real Christmas Grinch. Will this unplanned fiasco be the start of something magical?

Billionaire Holiday Romance Series

Driving Home for Christmas

The Valentine Getaway

Cruising Love

A Holiday Romance series because every holiday is special...

Read more at www.lexytimms.com.

Also by Lexy Timms

12 Days of Christmas
Snowflake Hollow - Part 1

A Bad Boy Bullied Romance
I Hate You
I Hate You A Little Bit
I Hate You A Little Bit More

A Bump in the Road Series
Expecting Love
Selfless Act
Doctor's Orders

A Burning Love Series
Spark of Passion
Flame of Desire
Blaze of Ecstasy

A Chance at Forever Series
Forever Perfect
Forever Desired
Forever Together

A Dark Mafia Romance Series
Taken By The Mob Boss
Truce With The Mob Boss
Taking Over the Mob Boss
Trouble For The Mob Boss
Tailored By The Mob Boss
Tricking the Mob Boss

A Dating App Series
I've Been Matched
You've Been Matched
We've Been Matched

A "Kind of" Billionaire
Taking a Risk
Safety in Numbers
Pretend You're Mine

A Maybe Series

Maybe I Should
Maybe I Shouldn't
Maybe I Did

Assisting the Boss Series
Billion Reasons
Duke of Delegation
Late Night Meetings
Delegating Love
Suitors and Admirers

BBW Romance Series
Capturing Her Beauty
Pursuing Her Dreams
Tracing Her Curves

Beating the Biker Series
Making Her His
Making the Break
Making of Them

Betrayal at the Bay Series
Devil's Bay
Devil's Deceit
Devil's Duplicity

Billionaire Banker Series
Banking on Him
Price of Passion
Investing in Love
Knowing Your Worth
Treasured Forever
Banking on Christmas
Billionaire Banker Box Set Books #1-3

Billionaire CEO Brothers
Tempting the Player
Late Night Boardroom
Reviewing the Perfomance
Result of Passion
Directing the Next Move
Touching the Assets

Billionaire Hitman Series
The Hit
The Job
The Run

Billionaire Holiday Romance Series
Driving Home for Christmas
The Valentine Getaway
Cruising Love

Billionaire Holiday Romance Box Set

Billionaire in Disguise Series
Facade
Illusion
Charade

Billionaire Secrets Series
The Secret
Freedom
Courage
Trust
Impulse
Billionaire Secrets Box Set Books #1-3

Blind Sight Series
See Me
Fix Me
Eyes On Me

Branded Series
Money or Nothing
What People Say
Give and Take

Building Billions
Building Billions - Part 1
Building Billions - Part 2
Building Billions - Part 3

Butler & Heiress Series
To Serve
For Duty
No Chore
All Wrapped Up

Change of Heart Series
The Heart Needs
The Heart Wants
The Heart Knows

Counting the Billions
Counting the Days
Counting On You
Counting the Kisses

Cry Wolf Reverse Harem Series
Beautiful & Wild
Misunderstood

Never Tamed

Darkest Night Series
Savage
Vicious
Brutal
Sinful
Fierce

Diamond in the Rough Anthology
Billionaire Rock
Billionaire Rock - part 2

Dirty Little Taboo Series
Flirting Touch
Denying Pleasure
Forbidding Desire
Craving Passion

Dominating PA Series
Her Personal Assistant - Part 1
Her Personal Assistant - Part 2
Her Personal Assistant Box Set

Fake Billionaire Series

Faking It
Temporary CEO
Caught in the Act
Never Tell A Lie
Fake Christmas
Fake Billionaire Box Set #1-3

Firehouse Romance Series
Caught in Flames
Burning With Desire
Craving the Heat
Firehouse Romance Complete Collection

Forging Billions Series
Dirty Money
Petty Cash
Payment Required

For His Pleasure
Elizabeth
Georgia
Madison

Fortune Riders MC Series
Billionaire Biker
Billionaire Ransom

Billionaire Misery
Fortune Riders Box Set - Books #1-3

Fragile Series
Fragile Touch
Fragile Kiss
Fragile Love

Great Temptation Series
The Devil's Footsteps
Heaven's Command
Mortals Surrender

Hades' Spawn Motorcycle Club
One You Can't Forget
One That Got Away
One That Came Back
One You Never Leave
One Christmas Night
Hades' Spawn MC Complete Series

Hard Rocked Series
Rhyme
Harmony
Lyrics

Heart of Stone Series
The Protector
The Guardian
The Warrior

Heart of the Battle Series
Celtic Viking
Celtic Rune
Celtic Mann
Heart of the Battle Series Box Set

Heistdom Series
Master Thief
Goldmine
Diamond Heist
Smile For Me
Your Move
Green With Envy
Saving Money

Highlander Wolf Series
Pack Run
Pack Land
Pack Rules

Hollyweird Fae Series
Inception of Gold
Disruption of Magic
Guardians of Twilight

How To Love A Spy
The Secret
The Secret Life
The Secret Wife

Just About Series
About Love
About Truth
About Forever
Just About Box Set Books #1-3

Justice Series
Seeking Justice
Finding Justice
Chasing Justice
Pursuing Justice
Justice - Complete Series

Karma Series

Walk Away
Make Him Pay
Perfect Revenge

Kissed by Billions
Kissed by Passion
Kissed by Desire
Kissed by Love

Leaning Towards Trouble
Trouble
Discord
Tenacity

Love on the Sea Series
Ships Ahoy
Rough Sea
High Tide

Lovers in London Series
Risking Millions
Venture Capital
Worth the Expense
The Price of Luxury

Love You Series
Love Life
Need Love
My Love

Managing the Billionaire
Never Enough
Worth the Cost
Secret Admirers
Chasing Affection
Pressing Romance
Timeless Memories
Managing the Billionaire Box Set Books #1-3

Managing the Bosses Series
The Boss
The Boss Too
Who's the Boss Now
Love the Boss
I Do the Boss
Wife to the Boss
Employed by the Boss
Brother to the Boss
Senior Advisor to the Boss
Forever the Boss
Christmas With the Boss
Billionaire in Control
Billionaire Makes Millions

Billionaire at Work
Precious Little Thing
Priceless Love
Valentine Love
The Cost of Freedom
Trick or Treat
The Night Before Christmas
Gift for the Boss - Novella 3.5
Managing the Bosses Box Set #1-3
Managing the Bosses Novellas

Mislead by the Bad Boy Series
Deceived
Provoked
Betrayed

Model Mayhem Series
Shameless
Modesty
Imperfection

Moment in Time
Highlander's Bride
Victorian Bride
Modern Day Bride
A Royal Bride
Forever the Bride

Mountain Millionaire Series
Close to the Ridge
Crossing the Bluff
Climbing the Mount

My Best Friend's Sister
Hometown Calling
A Perfect Moment
Thrown in Together

My Darker Side Series
Darkest Hour
Time to Stop
Against the Light

Neverending Dream Series
Neverending Dream - Part 1
Neverending Dream - Part 2
Neverending Dream - Part 3
Neverending Dream - Part 4
Neverending Dream - Part 5
Neverending Dream Box Set Books #1-3

Outside the Octagon

Submit
Fight
Knockout

Protecting Diana Series
Her Bodyguard
Her Defender
Her Champion
Her Protector
Her Forever
Protecting Diana Box Set Books #1-3

Protecting Layla Series
His Mission
His Objective
His Devotion

Racing Hearts Series
Rush
Pace
Fast

Regency Romance Series
The Duchess Scandal - Part 1
The Duchess Scandal - Part 2

Reverse Harem Series
Primals
Archaic
Unitary

Roommate Wanted Series
The Roommate

R&S Rich and Single Series
Alex Reid
Parker
Sebastian

Saving Forever
Saving Forever - Part 1
Saving Forever - Part 2
Saving Forever - Part 3
Saving Forever - Part 4
Saving Forever - Part 5
Saving Forever - Part 6
Saving Forever Part 7
Saving Forever - Part 8
Saving Forever Boxset Books #1-3

Secrets & Lies Series
Strange Secrets
Evading Secrets
Inspiring Secrets
Lies and Secrets
Mastering Secrets
Alluring Secrets
Secrets & Lies Box Set Books #1-3

Shifting Desires Series
Jungle Heat
Jungle Fever
Jungle Blaze

Sin Series
Payment for Sin
Atonement Within
Declaration of Love

Southern Romance Series
Little Love Affair
Siege of the Heart
Freedom Forever
Soldier's Fortune

Spanked Series
Passion
Playmate
Pleasure

Spelling Love Series
The Author
The Book Boyfriend
The Words of Love

Strength & Style
Suits You, Sir
Tailor Made
Perfect Gentleman

Taboo Wedding Series
He Loves Me Not
With This Ring
Happily Ever After

Tattooist Series
Confession of a Tattooist
Surrender of a Tattooist
Heart of a Tattooist

Hopes & Dreams of a Tattooist

Tennessee Romance
Whisky Lullaby
Whisky Melody
Whisky Harmony

The Bad Boy Alpha Club
Battle Lines - Part 1
Battle Lines

The Brush Of Love Series
Every Night
Every Day
Every Time
Every Way
Every Touch
The Brush of Love Series Box Set Books #1-3

The City of Mayhem Series
True Mayhem
Relentless Chaos
Broken Disorder

The Debt

The Debt: Part 1 - Damn Horse
The Debt: Complete Collection

The Fire Inside Series
Dare Me
Defy Me
Burn Me

The Gentleman's Club Series
Gambler
Player
Wager

The Golden Game
On The Pitch
Respect the Game
All Game
Sweat and Tears

The Golden Mail
Hot Off the Press
Extra! Extra!
Read All About It
Stop the Press
Breaking News
This Just In

The Golden Mail Box Set Books #1-3

The Lucky Billionaire Series
Lucky Break
Streak of Luck
Lucky in Love

The Millionaire's Pretty Woman Series
Perfect Stranger
Captive Devotion
Sweet Temptations

The Sound of Breaking Hearts Series
Disruption
Destroy
Devoted

The University of Gatica Series
The Recruiting Trip
Faster
Higher
Stronger
Dominate
No Rush
University of Gatica - The Complete Series

T.N.T. Series
Troubled Nate Thomas - Part 1
Troubled Nate Thomas - Part 2
Troubled Nate Thomas - Part 3

Toxic Touch Series
Noxious
Lethal
Willful
Tainted
Craved
Toxic Touch Box Set Books #1-3

Undercover Boss Series
Marketing
Finance
Legal

Undercover Series
Perfect For Me
Perfect For You
Perfect For Us

Unknown Identity Series

Unknown
Unpublished
Unexposed
Unsure
Unwritten
Unknown Identity Box Set: Books #1-3

Unlucky Series
Unlucky in Love
UnWanted
UnLoved Forever

War Torn Letters Series
My Sweetheart
My Darling
My Beloved

Wet & Wild Series
Stormy Love
Savage Love
Secure Love

Worth It Series
Worth Billions
Worth Every Cent
Worth More Than Money

You & Me - A Bad Boy Romance
Just Me
Touch Me
Kiss Me

Standalone
Wash
Loving Charity
Summer Lovin'
Love & College
Billionaire Heart
First Love
Frisky and Fun Romance Box Collection
Beating Hades' Bikers
Everyone Loves a Bad Boy
Dead of Night

Watch for more at www.lexytimms.com.

About the Author

"Love should be something that lasts forever, not is lost forever." Visit USA TODAY BESTSELLING AUTHOR, LEXY TIMMS https://www.facebook.com/SavingForever *Please feel free to connect with me and share your comments. I love connecting with my readers.* Sign up for news and updates and freebies - I like spoiling my readers! http://eepurl.com/9i0vD website: www.lexytimms.com Dealing in Antique Jewelry and hanging out with her awesome hubby and three kids, Lexy Timms loves writing in her free time. MANAGING THE BOSSES is a bestselling 10-part series dipping into the lives of Alex Reid and Jamie Connors. Can a secretary really fall for her billionaire boss?

Read more at www.lexytimms.com.